AF434094

DEDICATION

To the people of Fiji, friends of Fiji and
all those who call Fiji home.

CONTENTS

Mr. Narain's Treasure

And Other Stories

PAULINI TURAGABECI AND KHEMENDRA KUMAR

Kulawai Press

Copyright © 2023 Paulini Turagabeci and Khemendra Kumar

The characters and events portrayed in this book are
fictitious. Any similarity to real persons, living or dead,
is coincidental and not intended by the author.
No part of this book may be reproduced, or stored in a
retrieval system, or transmitted in any form or by any means,
electronic, mechanical, photocopying, recording, or otherwise,
without express written permission of the publisher.

All rights reserved.

ISBN:978-982-101-475-5

ACKNOWLEDGMENTS

We wish to acknowledge our readers, our families, the University of the South Pacific Library Services, especially to Gwen Rounds, and all those who've had a hand at making us published Authors.

MR. NARAIN'S TREASURE

By Paulini Turagabeci

If you've ever been to a squatter settlement in Suva, you might find that you've chanced upon the most fascinating thing about the capital. Now, this assumption may not hold true for everyone, but it's one I'm prepared to lose a claw and incisor over.

Mind you, I've been places in Suva. Fancy places if you like. One time I snuck into the Tanoa Hotel on McGregor Road. You'd think the staff would be more vigilant. But I walked past the receptionist and the guard on duty as if I were invisible.

Of course, a slight oversight by the workers didn't mean I remained invisible forever. But by the time they chased me out, I had already experienced some of the finer luxuries of hotel living. I had curled up in the King-sized bed. I stretched and snuggled deeper into the soft mattress. It was almost like sinking into a sea of marshmallows. It was glorious.

Then, I watched a bit of TV, the pay-per-view

type with strange people who didn't look like locals. I wasn't much into it until I came upon a channel about pets. I was fascinated by how these strange people groomed their dogs. They looked far different from the mangy pot-belly strays in Suva's neighbourhoods.

One such dog had a bubble bath in her own special jacuzzi. She looked like candy floss after getting her hair blow-dried. She was even pink. Argh, I hate dogs.

Speaking of baths, I hate those too. I try to avoid them like women avoid men without money. So I didn't bother checking out the hot and cold showers with floors so polished the President could eat off them.

This isn't to say I'm the filthy type. On the contrary, my hygiene is impeccable, regardless of what you might think of me. Still not persuaded?

Well, I've even been to the iconic Grand Pacific Hotel, one of the oldest hotels in the South Pacific. Though built in the early 1900's for luxury loving cruise ship tourists, it didn't stop this land lover from breaching its perimetres. I stayed a whole week. I doubt any of the British Royals who came for a visit stayed that long.

But enough about hotels. I've been to Five Star Restaurants too. Not that they were awarded Michelin stars, but that social media five star reviews was enough to fill tables and slip bills into tills.

On one occasion, I went to the cosmetic section of a luxury mall. It's hard to describe the smell there. But I imagined a goddess gathering all the flowers in the world. She'd melt the petals in gold cauldrons and with delicate fingers, she'd garnish the concoction with diamonds. And then, with a whispered incantation, release the final product in fine mists of perfection.

But that's far from the truth. The perfume aisles smelled that way because random women came and sprayed themselves as if they were taking a shower. And not just from a single bottle. They went through as many bottles available. A man could faint from intoxication alone if he walked by.

The sales clerks watched on with silent distaste yet could not do anything but throw shade and pretend ignorance. The whole scene was fascinating to watch. Then someone grabbed me by the scruff of the neck and showed me the door.

Would you believe that? I was kicked out by one of the sales girls, or boy, I couldn't really tell. How very rude. Whatever faux pas I made in these grand places to deserve such inhospitality was lost on me.

However, I wasn't kicked out of a nightclub. I knew I would be unwelcome so I snuck in through an open toilet window. Besides, there was a long queue outside. But no sooner did I slip past a patron entering the restroom than I scurried back into the toilet and escaped through the windows again. The music was so insane it felt like it could murder me with its violent beats alone.

That was it. Suva's metropolis's fancy lights and high rise no longer impressed me. I had had enough. So I decided to explore the parts of town people lived and breathed, so to speak. I avoided gated communities with white-washed walls, polished windows, and immaculate gardens. The bigger the houses, the further away I looked.

One day, as I ambled along Mead Road, I was tempted to sneak into the type of home I had sworn never to enter. The longer I thought about it, the weaker my resistance. I couldn't resist the urge to get a shot of air conditioning against my sun struck face. The urge to listen to the hypnotic whir of an automatic washing machine was magnetic. I saw a house across the road and decided to pay it a visit. To *ieli* with road rules! I crossed without looking.

Beeeeeeeep! Beeeeeeep! My hackles rose. I turned to see an oncoming vehicle. The driver blared his horn so ferociously it reminded me of the music that attacked me in the nightclub. Trauma is a real thing. I jumped as if I stepped on a bed of thorns, then sprinted out of the way. I didn't think about where I was going. I didn't care that people called after me. Some concerned, some finding my fright entertaining.

When I finally came to a stop, it was almost as if I had stepped into an entirely different world. Gone were the cement homes with the posh cars parked on smooth white driveways. Gone were the security cameras, small and forbidding. Gone too were the monochromic walls the rich preferred.

Instead, I stood in a maze of colourful tin-walled homes, some rusty, some new. Others were wooden, not like the Cottage on Knolly Street, elegant and graceful. More like a collection of flotsam and jetsam rescued from a shipwreck and nailed together at odd angles that fit best. They had no rhyme or reason to their architecture. Their only purpose was to stand erect long enough for their inhabitants to make a life living under their protection.

One such inhabitant was a boy in a faded oversized t-shirt that covered his shorts. It almost looked like he was wearing a mini-dress. I liked him straight away. He liked me too because when our eyes met, we knew we would make great partners in crime. Sometimes intuition about friendship can be so uncanny. The boy had the curliest mass of hair on his head (that seemed misplaced on his tiny face) and a pair of large friendly eyes.

He introduced himself as Ayush Kaliopate Khan. He found my name too hard to pronounce and told me instead that I looked like a "Percy." I liked the name and responded to it willingly. This is where my tale actually starts.

Forgive me. As you can see from my loitering on Suva's streets, I've been known to meander about before getting to the point.

It was the school holidays when Ayush and I met. For this reason, the settlement of Rukuilovoni was noisy and busy. Ayush said the place would quiet down when the school term started again. It came to Ayush's family's attention that I was an orphan, and they generously welcomed me into their home.

While Ayush spent countless hours playing tyres and chasing his friends with sticks, what he liked best was hanging around the "big boys". He didn't need to be in on the big boys' conversation. He just wanted to be seen near them. It made him feel not so little because at twelve years old, he looked like he was only six.

The big boys as Ayush referred to them, were Liki, Nikhil, and Poni. They had tattoos that looked like road maps leading nowhere. They smoked suki all day and competed in spitting contests. When they decided to get hair cuts, they didn't look any better. Their hair cuts were the kind that started with the smaller number on the top, ridiculous fades on the side, with a remaining bush at the back of their heads. The candy floss dog looked better. Liki, Nikhil and Poni spent the better part of their day sitting on a concrete wall whose purpose was never entirely clear.

The wall faced the dwelling of a Mr. Narain. His home was fenced about by low cement walls and long metal bars. It was easy to see into the compound.

"Hey, Small," called Liki. Ayush responded with a wave. I began to wonder whether it was normal in these parts to call each other by monikers. They made-up names they thought fitted the other person instead of using their real name.

"Here, have some mango skin," said Liki. He appeared to be the best looking of the three, considering that he had a broken nose that hadn't healed quite right.

Ayush took the sweet enthusiastically and shared a piece with me. We both knew it was the leftover chaser from last night's baby mix. Anyway, it was unclear what Mr. Narain's trade was. But if his home was any indication of his occupation, it would have to be an impressive one.

For Mr. Narain's house was an anomaly among the makeshift shelter of us slum dwellers. It was a triple-story building, windows tinted black, walls plastered with decorative tiles, and those white steel boxes that hummed and blasted cool air to the interior. Air Condition. I sighed. *Wainidiva.*

"When I was born," said Liki, "Na said Mr. Narain's house was a one bedroom tin shack that didn't even have an indoor toilet." He took a deep drag of suki then spat a sharp arrow of saliva ahead of him.

"Yeah, but his house always smelled like a sweet shop," said lanky Poni. He reminisced out loud about the smell of fresh *jalebi, murku,* and *lakdi* that woke him up in the morning.

When Poni asked his mother to buy sweets from Mr. Narain, she told him the sweets would send him straight to the hospital, where he'd get his leg amputated. Then she'd ship him off to school with the greasiest fish and chips if it was a pay week. Or a sickly sweet jam sandwich on a non-pay week. The boys laughed at the irony of it all.

"But I'd use all my spending money buying laddoo's, barfi's, and bean tamarind from him," said Poni.

"Boy, those were the days," mused Nikhil. He was short and squat with a missing front tooth. He could spit wads of saliva out the gaping hole of his front teeth with great precision. Spider-man would be hard-pressed to aim his web-shooters as competently.

I sat listening in on the conversation as Ayush dug tiny drains into the dirt using the end of a stick. I knew he was listening attentively too. From what I heard from the big boys, Mr. Narain used to leave at the crack of dawn with a cart on wheels laden with sweets and savouries. The wheels allowed him to position himself close to would-be customers.

Mr. Narain's first stop was outside a school where he hawked his wares to children arriving in the morning. At midday, his wife brought him a roti parcel and hot tea for lunch and a basket of sweets to restock his supply.

Next, Mr. Narain stationed himself outside the local clinic and brought in good money from patients and medical staff alike. Then, before midafternoon, he wheeled his cart back to the school. He knew the kids still had loose change jiggling around in the pockets. But even then, many of the children still begged their parents to buy from Mr. Narain's cart.

Before long, Mr. Narain built a small extension to his home from which he opened a canteen. Mrs. Narain looked after the canteen while Mr. Narain went on his usual sweet cart rounds.

They sent their children to good schools from the money they made. They even enrolled them in Private Education at the International School for their senior years.

"It's that temple of his, I tell you," said Liki, "It brings him good luck."

Mr. Narain's temple grew as his house grew, making it large enough for a small family to live comfortably inside. There were idols of various gods in the temple. But Lord Krishna held paramount importance amongst them. A crucified Jesus balanced on his cross at the corner, and two Budha statues sat beside the doorway as if stationed as guards.

At night, the temple was lit with colourful fairy lights. The kind people only hung up on Christmas or Diwali.

"Then how about uncle Deo? He has a little altar outside his house, but he's still a *kanikani* mechanic who can't wake himself up in the morning. The whole settlement can hear aunty Pooja screaming at him to get out of bed," said Poni.

As the conversation continued, it was evident that the boys became more intrigued about how Mr. Narain, a man who started at the bottom of the slush pile just like them, was now living like a king.

They watched as Mr.Narain's electric gate slid open and his BMW coasted, almost floating like a noiseless hovercraft into the compound. Mr. Narain stepped out in a black suit and tie.

"I bet he's part of the Mafia now," said Nikhil.

"*Seti, seti, mafia ga o'io,*" cried his friends. They whooped and jested.

They didn't notice that Mr. Narain looked in their direction momentarily before disappearing indoors. It became the boys' pass time to find their way to the wall and gaze at Mr. Narain's house. If they were as dedicated to their school work as they were at studying the Narain's home, perhaps they could have lived as lavishly. But their endeavours finally paid off.

One day as Ayush and I made our way to dump the household refuse in the large overflowing yellow steel rubbish bin by the roadside, we passed the big boys. They talked urgently among themselves. Ayush and I wanted to know what all the fuss was about. They didn't seem to notice our approach.

"I woke up early this morning to watch Mr. Narain do his morning prayers," said Poni. He looked older than his 17 years with his increasing fondness for smoke and yaqona. His back, already hunched, stooped even further as he relayed what he saw to Liki and Nikhil.

"First, he picks flowers and places them on a silver tray," said Poni. "Then he goes into his temple and kneels before the blue statue."

"Lord Krishna," said Nikhil.

"Yes, that's the one. He lights two incense sticks and waves them in front of the statue. He also does this circular motion before the idol with the tray of flowers." Poni imitated the movement, palms spread side by side, balancing an imaginary platter in his hands.

"But that's not the strangest part," continued Poni conspiratorially.

His friends leaned closer, drawn into the suspense. "When he finishes his worship, Mr. Narain walks to the Avocado tree behind the temple. He crouches down to remove a rock from around the tree's roots. And guess what?"

"*Oso, qai cava*?" said Liki impatiently. Poni enjoyed holding his audience captive.

"*Io gona*, the rock covers a hole in the trunk. Mr. Narain reaches in and removes a small silver box. It looks like a woman's jewelry box, but I can't be too sure. He opens the box and stares inside for a while."

Nikhil almost kicked me in his excitement. "What was inside?"

Poni gave an exaggerated sigh. "Sorry, bro. I couldn't see. I was too far away. The only other thing I saw was him closing the box, putting it back into the tree, and replacing the stone in front of it. Then he went back inside."

"It could all be a coincidence," said Liki, "What do you say, Small?"

Ayush only shrugged and smiled.

"Let's see if he does it again tomorrow and the next day and the next," said Liki. "If he does, then there must be something special about what's in that box."

"Treasure," said Nikhil and Poni in unison. And

they broke out in laughter.

The boys decided to watch Mr. Narain's daily routine. It wasn't easy for any of them to wake up early, so it was just as well that they took turns.

Ayush and I were excited to return every day to hear the latest development. And each day, the boy on watch duty reported the same thing. After finishing his morning devotions at the temple, Mr. Narain went to the Avocado tree, removed the stone, retrieved the silver box, stared at its content, then replaced it inside the tree hollow.

"It's some sort of treasure, I tell you," said Nikhil. "Why else would he keep it hidden? Why else would he check up on it every day?"

"Not just any treasure," added Poni. "It must be some magical sort of treasure. One that makes him so rich."

"I'd like that treasure," said Liki, gazing longingly at the Avocado tree. And then his eyes lit up in mischief.

"We should take it."

"That's stealing," said Ayush, more matter-of-fact than accusatory.

"Okay fine," said Liki, "Why don't we find out what's inside the box first. Then, if we like it, we'll take it. But I just have to know what's inside. Not knowing is eating me up."

The boys now had a glimpse of purpose to their existence. They decided they would find a way to get to Mr. Narain's treasure. It might have been the only thing they ever put their minds to.

"We just have to figure out how to get inside the compound," said Liki.

Getting inside would be no easy task. Mr. Narain had an automated gate. Every morning before he drove out in his BMW, Mr. Narain opened his gate to let out his dogs, Rocket and Bazuka. The dogs relieved themselves and stretched their legs outside the compound. They were large, aggressive dogs, and it didn't help that they didn't like most of the neighbours. Especially children, and teenagers. Liki and Nikhil were fond of antagonising the canines when they passed by Mr. Narain's closed gate. Sometimes they ran a stick along the metal bars to get the dog's attention. Then, when the dogs barked at them, they would hurl insults at Rocket and Bazuka and rile them up even further.

"Those dogs hate me," said Nikhil. "They'd be on me before I got a leg in."

"Hey, I have an idea," said Liki. His eyes shone as he looked at Ayush.

"How would you like to go on an adventure, Small?"

Ayush was eager to please the big boys. Doing them this favour would really make him one of them. The big boys agreed that they would hoist Ayush up over the fence in the early hours of the morning. It would still be dark enough to keep suspicious eyes away. Ayush would hide out in the temple, which was left unlocked. He was small enough to conceal himself behind any one of the large idols.

I wondered why he couldn't just go straight to the avocado tree to retrieve the treasure until I heard Poni say, "Stay in the temple until Mr.Narain goes to work and lets his dogs out. It will be bright enough that the motion detector lights won't go off and alert them about movement in the compound."

Ayush was restless with anticipation the whole night. He couldn't sleep, and neither could I. Then, at around 3 am, the big boys came to Ayush's home. We heard the signal outside our window. Four slow raps on the window sill, followed by two rapid ones.

"You and I will get into the compound and see what's up. You'll need to be quick. I don't have a plan yet of how I'm going to find my way out again, but I'll figure it out when we're inside," said Ayush as we made our way to Mr. Narain's gate.

It was the worst plan anyone had the guts to carry out. But it was too late to back out now. Everything was stock-still. It only took one boy to hoist Ayush up because he weighed so little.

Once on the other side, Ayush led us to the temple door. It opened with a creak that scared us a smidge but wasn't enough to wake Rocket and Bazuka, who were asleep on Mr. Narain's porch. So much for guard dogs.

Inside the temple, it was dark. It smelled of incense and camphor. Some of the idols had eyes that popped out of their sockets, testament to the idol maker's level of prowess or lack thereof. Our hairs stood on hackles, so we drew closer to each other and kept our eyes shut.

We lay behind a large statue of Kali. I don't know why we chose her of all the available idols. She was the scariest looking one with her numerous hands ready for battle. But between her and the wall behind us, she was best positioned to give us the cover we needed.

We were just falling asleep when we heard the temple door open and footsteps enter. We knew it was Mr. Narain. Like me, Ayush hunkered down on all fours and risked a peek out from behind Kali's leg. The older man didn't notice that he had another two sets of eyes trained on him as he made homage to his gods. He struck a match and lit incense sticks. The smoke overpowered my nose, and I let out a sudden sneeze. Ayush spun on me and clasped a skinny hand over my mouth. Thankfully, the sound of Mr. Narain's bells masked my sneeze, and he didn't notice anything out of the ordinary.

We watched covertly as Mr. Narain pressed his palms together in prayer, above his head, then to his chest. He repeated these movements and prostrated himself before his gods as his lips moved in silent supplication.

"My dad is Muslim, and mum's a Catholic, but I've never seen anyone so devoted," Ayush whispered to me.

It must have only been a couple of minutes, but it felt like hours before Mr. Narain finally made his way out of the temple. We remained inside until we heard Mr. Narain open the gate. We watched as Rocket and Bazuka ran outside after the BMW.

"Come on, Percy, we have to go now," said Ayush.

We stepped outside just as Mr. Narain's tail end disappeared around the bend. The dogs would remain outside the property for a while before Mrs. Narain came out of the kitchen to call them back inside. We could make our way to the Avocado tree undetected. It was a simple matter of following the cement path laid on the ground, heading north of the compound.

Liki, Nikhil, and Poni watched us from the wall. They made hand signals at us that we couldn't decipher. But we didn't need to because we finally arrived at the Avocado tree unscathed. This was it, the moment of reckoning. Ayush leaned down and removed the rock. He reached inside the trunk until he pulled out the jewelry box.

I watched and waited with bated breath. Then I noticed a look of confusion trot across Ayush's face. It made me want to look into the box myself. But before I could satisfy my curiosity, I was cut off by the vicious barks from Rocket and Bazuka. It was every intruder for himself. I scrambled up the tree faster than lightning could strike an unsuspecting man.

As for Ayush, he thought of the box ahead of himself, shoving it back inside the tree trunk before screaming like a hungry newborn and hightailing it all around Mr. Narain's grounds. I watched helplessly as Rocket and Bazuka gained on my friend.

One dog bit at his shorts and tore right through them until only Ayush's skin was visible underneath. Mrs. Narain ran outside, shouting rapid Fiji-Hindi and brandishing a spatula. Then she whistled a sharp tune that made Rocket and Bazuka come to an immediate standstill. They trotted towards her like baby lambs, harmless and demure.

But Ayush failed to realise that the chase was over. He continued screaming, even as he found the superhuman agility to scale the gate.

Neither Ayush nor I will ever forget that day or that night when Ayush got the biggest hiding of his life at the end of a hosepipe. Later, Ayush and his parents paid a visit to Mr. Narain to give a formal apology. When they asked Ayush why he had been on the property, Ayush remained silent. They put it down to his traumatic experience with Rocket and Bazuka.

As punishment, Ayush was made to scrub Mr. Narain's driveway and rake his compound every day for a week. But he never cast his eyes on the Avocado tree that stood tall and mocked him. He never hung around the big boys again despite their attempts to make him tell them what he had seen.

Many years later, Mr. and Mrs. Narain sold their house and went abroad to retire with one of their daughters. None of their children remained in the country any longer. Mr. Narain sold the house at a lucrative price.

Everyone at Rukuilovoni was inquisitive to see their prospective new neighbour. Liki, Nikhil, and Poni, who were now fathers but still lived an aimless existence around the grog bowl or anywhere they could pass their time talanoa-ing, were the most excited. Perhaps Mr. Narain had left his treasure behind. After all these years, maybe they could finally get their hands on it.

The new neighbour was a Mr. Kumar. He was Ayush's Professor at Law School. It happened that

Ayush told him about the house up for sale.

Ayush still lived at home, but was in his final year of studies. Mr. Kumar invited Ayush one day for tea. I was invited along too. Mr. Kumar liked my type.

When Liki, Nikhil, and Poni found out, they said, "Now's your chance, Small. You can finally bring us the treasure."

After tea, Ayush told Mr. Kumar, "Many years ago, I saw a box hidden inside the Avocado tree. I wonder if it's still there?"

We went to the Avocado tree and retrieved the box. "It's just as I remember it," said Ayush.

He took out a piece of paper and handed it to Mr. Kumar. Ayush said, "I couldn't read it back then. But I remembered every letter placement and wrote it on a piece of paper when I got home. I told myself I'd work hard at reading so I could understand what was written on it."

When we left Mr. Kumar's home, the big boys, who didn't seem so big now, were waiting for us impatiently.

"So, did you get it?"

Ayush handed them the box without a word. Then we walked away. Behind us, we heard the men reading out the words in Mr. Narain's handwriting.

"Hard work beats talent when talent doesn't work

hard."

Something told me they never did believe that piece of paper was Mr. Narain's treasure. "The old man must have taken the real treasure with him," said Liki.

"Some people will never get it, will they, Percy?" said Ayush. He picked me up, for I was not as fast and nimble as I once was.

"Meow," I replied.

A BUCKET OF BISCUITS

By Paulini Turagabeci

Leba's love for her biscuit buckets was second only to her seven children, though some might argue otherwise. She collected buckets of all kinds with a passion. But on the day that Leba's love for her biscuit buckets turned to hate, a rooster crowed at 3am. She knew because she pressed the indented number 5 on the old button phone retrieved from under her pillow. The screen lit up. 3am. She groaned then cussed the rogue rooster.

It was much too soon to be dragged out of bed, especially by a rooster in the city. 4am was the official start to Leba's day. At least the rooster didn't crow in the middle of the night, she thought as she turned over to her side. That would have meant spirits roamed the ground...perhaps they were looking for a new soul to add to their ranks. That was Leba's last thought before she succumbed once more to the enticement of sleep, tucking the sandy haired head of her seventh child in the crook of her arm.

Leba loved her seven children the way she loved

her mass collection of empty buckets of biscuits. She had an order of preference with her children as she did her buckets. But it was the duty of a parent to keep this a secret.

Although Leba was not affectionate with words and motherly caresses towards them, like the airbrushed mothers on her outdated box TV, she would fight tooth and nail if her children were ever threatened.

That had never happened anyhow, so Leba did what most women who left family planning to the will of the man upstairs did - she fed and sheltered them enough to survive. Then escaped to the sea to get them out of her afro Fijian hair.

It was the sea that had introduced Leba to the exceptional uses for biscuit buckets. As a young newlywed living in her husband's village, the women often went to sea to collect sea urchins, shellfish, sea grapes and fish.

But buckets were also used in other facets of village life. The women carried their clothing to the river in their buckets to wash household linen. Biscuit buckets were used to water their gardens, milk the cow, store rice, sugar and flour. And biscuit buckets were used to carry vegetables into the nearest town to sell so they could buy their non-perishables.

One day when Leba had three extra male mouths

to feed under the roof that she shared with her in-laws and two unmarried sister-in-laws, Leba took her buckets out to gather food from the sea. She brought back two bucket loads of *tadruku, cawaki, dio, nama* and *lumi.* But her anticipation of a warm celebrated welcome for her industriousness was foiled by a sour reception from her mother-in-law.

"Take it back right now. It's too much. Empty half a bucket into the sink and throw the rest back into the sea," said the older woman.

Leba wanted to rage against her mother-in-law. But it was culturally incorrect. Instead, it was the motivation she needed to break rank and search for independence for her and her young family.

Six short months later, and aided by her skill for constant nagging, Leba convinced her husband to move to the city.

So they left with the clothes on their backs, and all their belongings packed in four trusty biscuit buckets. They headed for Suva city. There they made their home in an ever expanding squatter settlement built of corrugated iron and nick nacks.

On the day that Leba's love for her biscuit buckets turned to hate, most of Suva city was in its second day of water cuts. Folks at the Water Authority were working around the clock to replace the burnt transfer switch that threw the capital into immobility.

Leba felt the prickly feeling that crawled over her skin when she was away from the sea for too long. She postponed going because of the water cuts. It was one thing to appreciate the sea - quite another to sleep with the ocean still clinging to your body.

She sat at the weathered long red and white checkered tablecloth with her seven children. Leba fed her children a breakfast staple of biscuits that now lay in heaps on plastic plates. The plates were arranged in two parallel lines along both sides of the tablecloth. The biscuits came labeled "Breakfast Crackers" in large and small buckets, blue or white and single packages too. But that was a mouth full - Bisikete was its household name.

Samu, Leba's husband, lay snoring gently in the corner of the small living room of their two bedroom house. Leba saw him from the kitchen doorway as he turned on his back. Arms sprawled, his flaky right leg almost knocked over the last ember of the mosquito coil. A thin wisp of smoke snaked its way up in a lazy haze, before it disappeared through some spider webs near the ceiling.

Samu's snoring grew louder, evidence of exhaustion from his usual Friday night yaqona drinking with that good for nothing wife beater Jolame. Leba suspected the duo washed the yaqona down with Niko's home brew. Both men were spitting images of each other, in that money ran away from them like a mynah bird flees from a mongoose. Yet they always had enough to splurge on cheap drink.

There was a light drizzle outside, soon to turn into a downpour. Despite the water cuts, the customary Suva city rain supplied enough for a day's worth of drinking water and a full pot of tea. Leba's children had collected water from the single gutter that ran along one side of their roof. The rain travelled down the spout to the bucket at the bottom. Inside the house, 12 buckets were arranged like an obstacle course to catch the droplets that leaked from the roof.

Leba eyed the buckets with admiration. They were returning her the favour of giving them a home. Two of the buckets had been used to carry cement to fill the floors of a neighbour's new home. The workers discarded the buckets after their project was complete and Leba had the painstaking job of scraping off the dried muck with her knife.

Three of the buckets were from the six month ration of biscuits it took to feed her family of nine.

Another two belonged to her sister who came to visit them from the village. The buckets came loaded with oranges. On her sister's departure Leba gave her two stripe bags in exchange for the buckets.

The two with chipped rims were ones she found on the roadside. They had stunk of rotten food and household refuse even after the rubbish collectors had dumped their contents into the weekly rubbish trucks headed for the landfill. Their owners would have returned to find their make-shift trash can stolen. Leba considered it long term borrowing. Just like the other three she had "borrowed" from her neighbours' front yards.

She numbered the seat of every bucket along with her initials L.T. No one could ever argue that they were not legitimately hers.

Leba's children sat in order of seniority at breakfast. Except Ema who sat at the bottom of the old red and white checkered tablecloth. She poured scalding lemon leaf tea into piala's and passed it up to the others. The "bottom of the table cloth" was always nearest the closest exit. And almost always reserved for the older girls of a household.

Ema was the fourth child, the first born girl and the first of Leba's children born in the city. Her parents had hoped she had been born right after the first born, to balance out the gender scale. The real silent reason was more pronounced. A family needed a girl to help carry a mother's burden; to cook, clean, wash, serve and be-at-the-ready to run to do everyone else's bidding.

For her father, Ema's tardiness which was no fault of her own of course, made her arrival even sweeter. She was her father's *gone toko* from the time the hospital ultrasound returned inconclusive. Her father knew instinctively she was a girl. And Ema remained her father's favourite child even after the next three children came along.

But by the time Ema arrived, her mother resented her. For by now Leba was too wide around the waist, her arms competed in thickness with her legs and her once pert breasts had doubled in size and shrivelled in elasticity.

And Leba silently blamed her daughter for her third son's effeminate disposition. Perhaps if Ema had followed the expected hierarchy of birth, Epineri would not have gladly taken on the role of daughter; refusing to join his brothers in a boisterous show of brawn. He preferred instead to *vacakulei* his mother's hair in search of head lice which, try as she might, Leba couldn't refuse.

Epineri, who would later in life take on the grand persona of a drag-queen named Epicia also found ways to turn down a game of touch rugby with other boys in the settlement, insisting instead that he had to work on an urgent school assignment. Everyone took his word for it. But anyone who cared to put in the time for some sleuthing would soon find Epi in the kitchen observing his mother caramelize sugar in coconut milk for *purini*.

When the dry ingredients were mixed into the caramel, Epineri eagerly greased the insides of empty mackerel cans with butter. The cans would hold the *purini* mixture as they steamed in a pot of boiling water.

Last came baby Mike; two years old, the youngest of the brood and his mother's favourite. Fair skinned with large blonde curls and eyes the colour of desert sand, Mike was the cherub of the family and took after none of his immediate kin. Only, his paternal grandmother. He had her wide lips.

The women who had past disagreements with Leba over biscuit buckets snickered amongst themselves, "Must not be Samu's," said the one who accused Leba of stealing a bucket carrying a germinating sandalwood tree outside her front door, "the child looks nothing like him."

"It's all that yaqona she drinks, I tell you," argued Mrs. Vosalevu, who had an outstanding debt of $80 to pay Leba. "Between the two of them, husband and wife can finish a bucket a day."

If Leba had heard the gossip, she would have to agree with the latter. It was common knowledge that yaqona drinkers produced pale children, no matter their parents dark colouring. That's what her cousin Sala did during pregnancy - drank three bowls a day until she popped out an infant a shade darker than an albino. The child was ballyhooed as the beauty of the village despite its learning disabilities.

In her defence, Leba would argue that at least she did not smoke. Leba scorned the women who gathered at grog parties smoking like cigarette smoke was oxygen and air the toxin. She on the other hand was repulsed, thanks to the pamphlets distributed by the Ministry of Health containing graphic pictures of newborns with birth defects. Surprisingly enough, most babies born to those smoking mothers turned out alright.

But in a sardonic twist of fate, it was her child, the one not exposed to cigarette smoke who turned out...different. She didn't have a name for it but Mike was fidgety, impulsive, unable to play quietly on his own. He was only intrusive and extremely hyper. Albeit, they were traits found in all children to varying degrees, none of Leba's older children displayed it to the extent Mike did. Psychiatrists would have diagnosed it as ADHD, but Leba, like all Fijian women she knew, put it down simply as, "a little boy being a little boy."

Mike never got hand-me-downs from the older children. His clothes were always brand new or at least scavenged from the new stock of Suva's countless second hand clothing stores. Mike had never been spanked around the calves with the handle of a *Taufale*. Adriu, the second eldest child, held the record for that. And Mike had the largest first birthday party his parents could afford in comparison to his siblings.

Baby Mike sat on his special chair dangling his feet over the edge. They had a ways to go before they could reach the ground. His special chair was a bucket of biscuits. There were a few biscuits left in them. Enough for another day's breakfast. The bucket had Mike's red handprint on the side, marking it as his. It was both his special chair and naughty chair when keeping him under control was like catching a whirlwind.

Mike had had his breakfast before the others, the evidence of which was a wet neckline and traces of biscuit crumbs in the corners of his mouth and butter in his small palms. He cried for another buttered biscuit and Ema obliged him.

"Come up and sit here, Epineri," scolded Leba, "you're not a girl to be serving the tea."

After setting the pot of cassava over the fire, Epineri had sat at the bottom of the tablecloth and temporarily took over Ema's task. He huffed and strutted like a Fiji Fashion Week model until he came to his vacant spot. He dumped himself next to the eldest; 21 year old Koli who sat at the top end of the tablecloth, decked in overalls, ready to leave for the garage.

Adriu sat opposite Epineri. Pita, sat one rank down from Epineri and opposite Pita sat his twin sister Mele, who siddled close to her mother.

The knock on the door came as no surprise. It was a girl, no more than eight. She wore an overly large t-shirt hung loosely to one side, revealing her scrawny shoulder.

"Nau Leba, Mum would like to borrow four buckets please. We're expecting water trucks today."

Leba looked at the young girl and remembered a similar promise the girl's mother, Dai, had made, "Leba I'm going to the island. Give me seven buckets to bring kota in and I'll give you two buckets of kota in return."

Leba thought the deal was lucrative. She had a particular liking of the Lauan condiment made of finely scraped coconuts fermented in sea water. What was more lucrative was her eagerness to pack the kota into little plastic sachets, pair them with a handful of sea grapes, and sell them for $2 a heap at the Suva Municipal Market.

But what should have been a month's visit to the island, turned into an eight month hiatus. And when Dai returned, she had neither buckets nor kota for Leba. Apparently, eight months away had nullified the deal.

Ema rushed to retrieve the buckets before her mother could refuse. The newest buckets were stored under her bed. Buckets hired for manual labour like mopping, carrying crops from the plantation,or storing food scraps for dogs and pigs were kept in the boys room. The ones for everyday hire were kept in all four corners of the living room, where her mother could keep an eye on them even in her sleep. They were stacked until they rose like the long foundation pillars of a chief's house.

Leba watched on as the girl handed Ema $4 and the exchange was made. She turned to leave, but Leba called after her, "Ei how long will you be keeping the buckets for?"

The young girl shrugged. She didn't know.

"I want it back, same time tomorrow. If not, that's another $4."

It was human nature perhaps to find reasons to acquire a thing when that thing was in abundance. And it was the same for Leba's buckets. When her neighbours found out about her bucket hoarding, they came up with multiple reasons for their sudden need to borrow buckets.

Like the widower who needed it to make lemonade that he sold at the Suva market. Another was Mrs. Lumisa who was trying to get a coconut virgin oil business off the ground and needed to send buckets to her village cooperative of women to store their cold presses.

Five houses down and two rows back was the single mother who resorted to bathing her triplets in buckets because they had broken the bathroom faucet. There was also the mother who needed to keep her newborn's laundry separate from the rest of the household, and Mr. Pani Deo who needed Leba's buckets to collect water from an ever leaking tap.

And then there was the neighbourhood's bootlegger, Niko who was a criminal at heart and a businessman at best. When his secretive business began to outgrow his resources, he approached Leba for some buckets under the guise that he needed them for some friendly yaqona drinking with his friends.

But Leba was not easily compelled to neighbourly generosity. Even the shark god Dakuwaqa did not need five buckets worth of yaqona poured out to him in homage.

"$200 dollars a bucket," said Leba, upon Niko's request.

Niko shouted in protest. No one would pay so much for a hand me down bucket, much less an empty one. But Leba did not budge. Any attempt from Niko to bargain would only drive the price up. In her opinion she was giving the bucket for free. $200 was the price for her silence for as long as Niko's home brewery saw the light of day.

When neighbours saw Niko wash out his growing collection of buckets, they did not hesitate to accuse his accomplice. But Leba ignored the tongue wagging and finger pointing. None of them put food on her tablecloth. And neither would they put in the effort of calling the police.

Leba's transaction with Niko had sparked the idea.

Leba cashed in on the community need and before long, anyone who approached the house to *kere vokete* was met with a sign nailed to their wriggly tin wall, **"BUCKETS FOR HIRE - $1/per day"**. Granted she lost friends and gained enemies who did nothing more than gossip about her business venture, the same continued to be return customers.

Business allowed Leba to buy the family's fridge, washing machine and a brushcutter for Adriu who had willingly dropped out of school to earn a living cutting grass in and around Vatuwaqa.

But despite her assets and her entrepreneurial spirit, Leba's roof leaked in more places than there were family members. Her louvre blades were missing and those that remained hung on for dear life, clutching at rusted frames. She didn't even have an indoor shower or toilet yet. And she let her husband know who was to blame.

"Samu, sa dede na kena turu tiko na vale qo!"

Her husband Samu was still sprawled on his back in the corner where his tobacco leaves and strips of newspaper sat bundled in plastic bags.

Samu gave a yawn as he stretched both his body and lungs, "There's no water. At least a leaking roof gives us water."

The more industrious Leba grew, the more time her husband spent smoking his rolled suki. He passed his days under the shade of the barren avocado tree inviting anyone who cared to share a bowl of yaqona with him. At night, when she needed her nerves calmed from a long day of motherhood, and if her husband was not itinerant, Leba joined him in a bowl or two... or more.

On the day that Leba's love for her biscuit buckets turned to hate, the water trucks arrived with a large hose attached to its cylinder of water, ready to dispose of its depths. The driver popped his horn, loud and long.

"Hurry children, grab your buckets."

There was a race of limbs to fetch buckets. But Ema had to clear the half-eaten breakfast before she could fetch hers. The children retrieved every bucket available.

"Ema look after Mike," instructed Leba.

"But where are you going?" asked Ema. She received her answer when she saw her mother gathering her old fishing buckets, inside which she dropped her fishing line and net.

Now that Leba was certain of water, the call of the sea was much too strong to resist.

So Leba left her wriggly tin home as her children crowded in around the water truck with their buckets. The whole settlement had gathered at the roundabout, most jostling for first dibs. Leba rolled her eyes at the pots, ice cream tubs and even a fridge storage container - all items brought to store water. Then she saw her torpid husband sitting under the barren avocado tree smoking tobacco leaves and watching the water gatherer's, and all her pride dissipated.

Leba returned only an hour after she left. The sea had been unkind and yielded no catch. But it wasn't the strong wind blowing the salty water in her eyes nor the broken bottle that cut through her canvas to pierce her heel that brought her home. She felt a sinking feeling in the pit of her stomach as she rested to pull the shard of glass from her skin. Her blood ran red against the grey of the dead coral on the shore. And then it ran cold. Perhaps it was just the wind but she had to get home. In the distance, the sound of sirens wailed.

Leba met Ema crying and swallowing down gulps as she came.

"It was an accident…"

"I was busy fetching water…"

"He didn't want to be carried…"

"I only left him for a second…"

All of Leba's senses were assaulted but she was able to sift through the melee to piece the puzzle together.

The whole community gathered at her house. An

officer in blue was talking to a distraught Epineri. Her outdoor bathroom was brimming with biscuit buckets just as she had imagined, standing in neat rows, filled with water.

Then there was the one bucket that shouldn't have been there. The one with a child's handprint in red. It too had been filled with water. But unlike the others, it lay toppled on its side and beside it, an unknown heap lay covered in a white sheet.

"They found him head first and legs in the air," she heard a neighbour say in a loud whisper.

"No one could save him," said Mrs. Vosalevu, eyes transfixed on the white sheet.

"It's her fault for having so many buckets."

On the day that Leba's love for her biscuit buckets turned to hate, her knees buckled, her head spun. Her palms grew clammy, her stomach lurched. And when that rogue rooster crowed, everything went black.

MY SON'S DREAM

By Khemendra Kumar

Sarwan was cremated three days ago.

Tonight, a well-known singer came to sing kirtans. The makeshift shed was full of people. A group of women encircled Sarwan's widow, who sat lifelessly. Men formed small circles around yagona basins and made conversations in between the songs. Kava flowed at regular intervals, wetting the dry throats of the grog gang.

Sant Kumar, Sarwan's father, sat leaning on a concrete wall of his house. In deep thought. His only son died. He died before him. He had to torch the pyre where Sarwan lay dead. Sant never blinked once while Sarwan's body burned to ashes. But he felt his soul burn along with his son. This feeling has come back to him hundreds of times ever since. With this feeling, millions of other thoughts cluttered his mind. Whenever he took control of those troubling thoughts, reality came to the fore. His only son died.

Sant kept staring at all these people. He didn't

recognise most of them. These were unfamiliar faces, no connection to him whatsoever.

"Maybe they knew Sarwan," Sant reasoned. After all, Sarwan was a taxi driver. He must have known these people. Knowing many people is good for business; how can he forget this? He was also a taxi driver some twenty years ago.

Sant shrugged off those thoughts. Again, he tried hard to recognise some men sitting near him in the crowd. The cataract in his left eye didn't help much though he could see reasonably well with his right eye. For the past two years, he has been waiting for his eye operation. A sudden fear gripped him. "How will I find my way in the dark? Who will take me to the hospital now? Sarwan is dead?"

With his good eye, he saw Sarwan's son, Neeraj, walking toward him. "Ajja, come and have your meal. You look exhausted," Neeraj said aloud, intending to be heard. Sant looked straight at Neeraj. He had the same sharp features as Sarwan. That square chin and the straight nose! Already, he had reached his father's shoulders. In a few years, Neeraj could have shared his father's responsibilities. Just like Sarwan ... who stood by him when their land lease expired and the family had to relocate from his place of birth.

It was some thirty years ago. That night was long and angry. Rain sprayed like bullets from a machine gun. Having no place to go, Sant erected a hovel in a squatter settlement overnight. In the dim light from a nearby house, they nailed something that became their home. Soaked and shivering, Sarwan stood by Sant while the rain washed his mother's tears.

That night transformed the village lad into a responsible man. The very next day, Sarwan went out and about seeking work. The idea of school was erased from his mind; school, education, and books meant nothing to him. Putting food on the table was his aim now. But what work would he get? He was only fourteen! A kind man gave him a job at a car wash center. In a week, Sarwan proved his worth. He worked diligently. Coming from a village, he hardly had any opportunity to sit in anyone's car, but now he got the chance to touch and feel some of the most expensive cars. Soon he learned the names of all the models that came to the center. He went on to learn the specifications and many more details.

When Sarwan was not washing cars, he was helping at a nearby tyre repair center for extra cash. The proprietors were kind enough to let Sarwan shuttle between the two establishments. They were impressed by Sarwan's sincerity. Little did they know Sarwan had an insatiable desire; he craved every opportunity to work on cars. He soon developed a passion for cars.

As a stroke of luck, Sant started driving a taxi. Imagine Sarwan's delight! He washed the taxi until it was spotless. The interior of the car always carried a sweet fragrance. Many customers praised Sant for keeping his taxi spick and span without knowing that it was not Sant's but Sarwan's effort.

Sarwan's obsession with cars didn't end with washing, changing tyres, or cleaning them; at night, before sleep, he would bring out his toy car from his jute bag to play with it. At an age when boys were interested in fancy clothes, video games, and so many other things, Sarwan had only one obsession–cars!

While toying around, Sarwan talked to the toy car of his dream. He dreamt of a home, a place he could say his own. In his dream home, his parents had a bedroom of their own. There was a living room, a kitchen with built-in cabinets, a proper bathroom and toilet, and many more commodities. In his dream, he would see himself adding a kitchen appliance or decorating the living room. He included some fancy stuff from those shops that sold assorted decors … all in his dream. Each day he managed to add something new and remove the old, but his dream never got old. Such was his dream.

At last, Sarwan realised some part of his dream. He saved enough money to buy a taxi. With his taxi, he worked day and night. Bit by bit, he saved enough to buy a small plot of land. Then he built a house on it that eventually became a home for his small family. His home was simple, yet warm enough. Whenever Sarwan had a few dollars to spare, he would buy an ornament to decorate his home.

Today in the driveway stood Sarwan's taxi: lifeless and cold since his death, the same taxi that throve with Sarwan's heartbeat. The taxi blew life into many of Sarwan's dreams. Alas, he lost his last breath in it. What a destiny!

A hundred thoughts were ruminating in his mind like a whirlwind. He was in his present, his past, and beyond. Suddenly, he thought of Sarwan's mother. She died three years ago. Squatter life didn't suit her; she missed her home in the village, the trees in the yard, chickens in the pen, goats in the shed, and Lali, her cow. Selling off Lali broke her heart. During the initial days in the squatter, she used to recall one thing or another. She died of a broken heart, not dengue fever, as the doctor claimed.

Now Sarwan was gone. Just when they started to enjoy the rewards of their laborious life, tragedy hit them again. Suddenly Sant realised that he had to look after the family. He felt the weight of the wall pressing on his shoulders. He looked around, bewildered.

Someone put a hand on his shoulders. Turning around, he saw a new face. This person introduced himself as Sanjay. He was a bystander who witnessed the incident. Yes, the accident! Sant held his hand tight and made him sit near him. There was a deafening silence between them though the dholakia drummed the dholak with all his might.

Sanjay was served a bowl of kava. Sant kept looking into his eyes, seeking some answers, while Sanjay tried to evade those questioning eyes. At last, Sant spoke, "you were there, naa."

The incident was fresh in Sanjay's mind. He saw it all. For Sanjay, the thought of an innocent person losing his life for someone else's recklessness was sickening. What bothered Sanjay more was the unpredictability of life. One moment, you are alive, and the next, you are gone, just like that! The death of Sarwan evoked existentialist questions in his mind. The duality of dharma and karma, life and death, and the fickleness of life flooded his mind. Was life meant to be lived like Sisyphus?

From the time of the incident, he hardly shared what he witnessed, except with the police officer, for apparent reasons. The gentle drizzle, the screeching of tyres, the fall of the woman, and then … what he couldn't forget was the pain in Sarwan's eyes when the stranger suddenly struck him. As a fish scooped out of the water, Sarwan gulped for his breath, opening and closing his mouth in despair. Sanjay couldn't erase that moment from his memory; no matter how much he tried to shake off that thought, the memory returned in waves until painful tears escaped his eyes.

At last, Sanjay spoke. He began telling how it happened. It was drizzling, and there was a traffic jam. Sarwan tried to cut the line and enter a lane on the right, and just then, a middle-aged woman crossed the street. The taxi moved, the woman slipped and fell in the middle of the road, people thought Sarwan had bumped her, two youths came from nowhere, one helped the woman stand up, the other punched Sarwan at the back of his right ear. When the commotion subdued, then we realised that Sarwan was unconscious. By the time he was taken to the hospital, he was dead. Police arrested the person who assaulted him, but the post-mortem report indicated death from a heart attack. Case closed!

Sanjay kept his narration brief, yet Sant visualised it all like Dhritarashtra. Although Sarwan's case was closed, a new leaf was turning in Sant's life.

Sant didn't realise when Sanjay left. He was whirling in his own world. Occasionally he drank a bowl of kava. His shaven head started to itch; he scratched hard, cursing the ritual. Someone suggested rubbing some ghee. In the corner of their small veranda, Sarwan's widow sat limp, eyes dull and dried of tears. He was well aware of her thoughts, "what would happen next? Their house is under the mortgage, the taxi needs repair, Neeraj is in form four, and she knew nothing apart from domestic duties." Her world turned upside down just with a blow, a blow from someone unknown. What could Sarwan have done to him? Did he cheat him? Swear at him, what? Sarwan, to whomsoever, was the gentlest soul, ever-smiling, reliable, and punctual. Maybe he was too punctual; he did not make HIM wait.

Again thoughts were running wild in Sant's mind. From funds to family matters to what he has to act on now. It was drumming in his mind, much louder than the dholak.

What he saw in the shed the following day froze him. Sant saw emptiness, vast emptiness in his small yard. The trodden grass turned yellow and in between two posts stood a ghostly figure in a dull white sari and veil, his daughter-in-law. All barren. They looked at each other bewildered but stood rooted as if tied to a cross. Tears rolled from their eyes; not a single sob was heard. The widow slumped to the ground, but Sant suddenly found new strength in his old limbs. He wiped his tears with the back of his palm and started pulling down the shed.

Neeraj rushed out of the house when he heard the clanging of the roofing irons. "Ajja, what are you doing?" he asked.

"Can't you see it! I am pulling down the shed," Sant replied.

"But the ritual isn't over yet," Neeraj opposed.

"It's over! No ritual will bring my son back. It's all over now. The faster we realise this, the better for us," Sant replied curtly. "Now, either help me or stare with those confused eyes."

Neeraj had enough drama. He agreed to help without more fuss. First went the roofing iron, then the poles, and finally the posts. Done away with the shed, he said, "Beti, I need a glass of water."

Then Sant walked inside the house and came out with his driving licence in hand. He called Neeraj and his mother, "we need to talk." Their talk was punctuated with pauses.

"What are you up to, Daddy?" Neeraj's mother broke her fast.

"We are going to get an appointment with an eye specialist," replied Sant calmly. "This cataract gotta go."

"And then?" Neeraj enquired.

"And then we will realise Sarwan's dream," responded Sant.

"But how Ajja," Neeraj asked.

"Look at that taxi! I will drive it as soon as I can see properly," replied Sant.

Although the three looked quiet and calm outwardly, a hundred volcanoes were roaring in their minds. It was not a time to mourn, but to live.

"Beti, Sarwan is gone, but his dream of a happy home for us remains. Look at these hands, they shivered when I held the matchbox to torch the pyre, but today they were as steady as a rock."

After another long pause, Sant concluded, "Sarwan died, not his dream."

THE TIDAL WAVE

By Paulini Turagabeci

Fifteen seconds...

"It's coming! The tidal wave is coming!" The right course of action to take at the approach of a tidal wave is to drop everything and head for the hills. But for the Sekoula family, things were different. They had survived many visits from the tidal wave. They learned how to break the rules and live to see another day.

"Gather the plates and the cutlery," said Anareta Sekoula, and her children followed her commands intuitively.

Ten seconds...

Little feet scampered over polished wooden floors. A pair of feet slipped on a rug, then quickly regained their balance to continue the mission.

"Be quick. It's coming closer. No Jone, leave the noodles. Pack the flour and sugar in the carton, then take it outside to the shed."

8-year-old Jone moved with speed and precision

as he balanced a carton in one hand and cradled a germinating sandalwood plant in the other. He let the door slam behind him in his haste to reach the shed. Anareta thought of her husband Lorima, who earned a small wage at the soap factory. It was her duty to save what she could from the merciless tidal wave.

Five seconds…

"Na, what about this?"

Anareta took a hurried look at what her second eldest child, Luisa, held in her hands. It was the new vase she bought a fortnight ago. The vase was the size of a toddler, blown from molten sand and blue crystals. Her daughter had a good eye. The vase had become Anareta's most prized possession. It was a rare purchase from her usual family shopping. It had been so hard to acquire. She saved up six months of cash leftover from their budget to buy it. The only problem was that decorative vases were made to attract attention, not hide from it. So, where could she keep it out of the tidal wave's reach?

Anareta looked about, eyes darting in a frantic dance. There was no time to store the vase satisfactorily. A high shelf was out of the question. It would fall into the tidal wave's clutches.

"That goes under the bed, Luisa. Be careful you don't drop it."

"I don't understand why you bother," said Isikeli,

Anareta's 17-year-old. He was the only child who didn't care to follow the drill. Instead, Isikeli lounged on the living room sofa, ears plugged up and eyes glued to the screen of his phone.

"Wait until you can afford to buy things," said Anareta. She knew her words fell on her son's distracted ears.

Anareta gave the house a quick scan. It was bare, the type of home a minimalist would praise. Yet nothing gave away the sense that it wasn't lived in. The tidal wave will hit at any moment, but it will leave with less this time around, Anareta thought. It was uncommon - no - it was outrageous for her to think that she could dictate terms and conditions to the tidal wave. Yet Anareta was determined that this time around, it would be different.

Three..

Two...

One...

"Children! Children! It's Bui Nele. Please help me with my things."

Anareta found herself bargaining with God - *Lord, please, please, not the vase. She can take the sofa or the fridge. Just don't let her see the vase.*

Luisa ran out the door on Anareta's cue. Jone followed close behind. Pete, the youngest, still in diapers, wriggled out of his mother's arms to join the welcoming party. Isikeli departed for the kitchen.

"Bui Nele! Bui Nele!" cried the children.

An older woman arrived at the Sekoula's doorstep after making the short but toilsome walk from the road. She kissed the children lightly over the top of their curled hair. By the time the small entourage entered the house, Bui Nele had divested the two bags of luggage in her possession, courtesy of the children's hospitality. The Sekoula children jostled over who would get the honour of bringing the bags in. Jone won out and reverently placed Bui Nele's bags in a clean corner. Bui Nele also dispensed all the complaints and excuses stored in her head, carefully prepared for the ears of her extended relatives in the city.

"Oh, my back." she winced. "If only it didn't give me such a hard time, I would have brought you two dozen coconuts. Kelemedi husked several dozens for the *Lotu ni vulavou*. But he insisted it would be cruel of him to allow an old lady like me to bring so many coconuts to the city - alone."

Anareta pasted a tight smile on her face. If she knew her husband's cousin well, he would not be hunched over the metal *moto* to husk a coconut nor the metal *sakalo* to scrape one coconut, let alone several dozen. Kelemedi was prone to constant bouts of laziness thanks to a penchant for watered-down kava and potent moonshine. Bui Nele pulled off her woolen jumper, a necessity of the early morning boat ride from the island but now quite a bothersome entanglement.

"Luisa, bring me a glass of water, *noqu lewa*," said Bui Nele.

"It's so hot in here. Perhaps you could install a ceiling fan."

Bui Nele looked up at an imaginary ceiling fan before her eyes trailed across the room and tried, without success, to glimpse covertly behind the bedroom doors that stood ajar. In the same instant, Anareta spotted her doilies arranged on the coffee table behind Bui Nele. She chided herself. Why had she forgotten to hide those? She had paid two dollars per class at the Sanatan Women's Group to learn how to make doilies. The plan was to sell them and supplement her husband's income. She had completed a set of six doilies. Her pace was picking up.

After handing Bui Nele a glass of water, Luisa returned to Jone, and the siblings continued their game of cards beside the coffee table. Their game grew boisterous. Anareta's stomach clenched. She didn't want the children to draw Bui Nele's attention lest the older woman spied the doilies and come up with an elaborate explanation of why she should have Anareta's needlework of crotcheted artistry.

"Your house looks emptier than I remember," said Bui Nele. Her eyes grew narrow as she looked about. Anareta wondered if her aunt-in-laws eyes were narrowed with suspicion over the empty-looking house.

A Fijian home was a shrine to life. Every wall space, every corner, and countertop must declare the occupants' achievements, memories, and keepsakes. Yet Anareta's home almost resembled the doomsdayer she watched on the documentary channel who gave away all his belongings and waited for the apocalypse, holed up in a bunker secreted from civilization.

Oh God, don't let her look behind her. Anareta moved uncomfortably on her haunches.

"It's really hot in here. Where's Luisa? Please get me another glass of water, dear," said Bui Nele as she continued her unreserved perusal. Anareta called her daughter before Bui Nele could turn around. She must not see those doilies.

"Luisa-" but Anareta was cut off mid-sentence.

"Bui Nele, bula," greeted Isikeli, coming to his mother's rescue. He entered from the kitchen, finally making an effort to engage with the family guest. But it was only short-lived. Isikeli accepted a quick kiss from Bui Nele. Then, he excused himself to head to a game of rugby with the neighbourhood boys.

"How tall and handsome you've grown," gushed Bui Nele at her teenage grand-nephew. Butter wouldn't melt in her mouth.

Isikeli chuckled at the compliment. Before he headed out the door, he turned to re-enact the claws of a tidal wave grabbing everything within its reach before dragging them out to sea. His charade was for his mother's eyes alone. When she shot him a deadly look, he ran out, mischief still planted on his face as his sibling's giggles echoed after him.

Bui Nele, oblivious of Isikeli's antics, sipped on the glass of water Luisa handed her. When she paused to take a breath, she said," Delicious!" an exaggerated compliment everyone who knew her came to be only too familiar with.

Brace yourself, Anareta warned herself. Bui Nele was a sweet-talker. She used inflated compliments as leeway to a request, a favor, or gesture of goodwill from her listeners.

"*Isa na makubuqu*, I didn't get you any sweets. You know I'm just a widow, surviving on the good graces of the government's meager pension."

Of all the things Anareta disliked about Bui Nele, her inconsideration toward her children made top of the list. Was a Jasons lolly at ten cents a piece from the corner shop so hard to get?

Yet subsequently, it gave Anareta insight into Bui

Nele's own relationship with her adult children. All her three daughters lived abroad and hardly visited their mother. Her eldest son, Akuila, spent the first three years of married life living with his mother. Then, after a near divorce, Akuila moved his family to Lautoka, where he could regulate contact with Bui Nele. It did wonders for his marriage.

Kelemedi, the youngest, had always been the favorite and, in being so, never saw the deficiencies in his mother's personhood like his older siblings. Unfortunately, this meant that Anareta's husband, Lorima, Bui Nele's brother's son, became the burden-bearer of sorts. But not because it was a cultural responsibility set in stone. Instead, Lorima never had the nerve to refuse a request from his aunt.

So soon, the requests grew into expectation, and expectation grew into habit. The last time Bui Nele paid the Sekoula family a visit, she had asked for money to buy Kelemedi an outboard motor. Kelemedi needed it for fishing. She promised to send over fresh fish every month in exchange for the money. Needless to say, there was never any fish because there was never any outboard motor. And Bui Nele never gave any reason why.

However, there was a clue of where the money disappeared when pictures turned up of Bui Nele proudly milking a cow she previously didn't own. Anareta's blood spat bubbles like the Savusavu hot springs. She marched to Lorima and stabbed the picture on her phone. "Is this why we send money? So your aunt can pick up a new hobby?"

There was an all-out war between husband and wife when Lorima insisted that Anareta forget about the issue.

"Just leave it. Don't ask about the money, the cow, or the outboard motor," said Lorima.

"Stop cowering under an old woman," Anareta retorted. In all her eighteen years of marriage to Lorima, Anareta never complained about the duties she took on for her husband's side of the family. As an indigenous woman, she had been prepared all her life. She remembered Mr. Kaukimoce's Vernacular and Social Science lessons from her Primary School days;

Reguregu: Derived from the word "to kiss", a sort of last farewell to the dead, where wealth of *ibe, masi, tabua* and yaqona are taken to the deceased's family.

Roqoroqo: The first visit to a newborn, derived from the word "to cradle" Lakovi: A formal request for a woman's hand in marriage

Kau Matanigone: Ceremonial first visit to a child's maternal side (Often reserved for the first born).

The list went on, and Anareta knew all this in theory. Yet it was her mother who had ushered her into practical learning. Anareta was never excused from a family function, a communal gathering of the extended family, or village ceremony.

You will leave your family and attach yourself to your husband's family. You must bear every communal burden with him. Don't let your husband's family think we didn't raise you well, were her mother's parting words before Anareta abandoned her maiden name, Bucaqiqo, and became Mrs. Sekoula.

Anareta readily accepted that to marry Lorima was, in some way, to marry his whole clan. Her only qualm was with Bui Nele. She never signed up to meet one woman's every need and demand.

A noise from the bedroom caught everyone's attention. Anareta tried to ignore it, fearing that the things purposefully hidden away would be revealed to their guest. But it was too late for concern, for two-year-old Pete waddled out with his mother's glass vase precariously balanced in his untrained toddler hands. He supported it with his whole body because it was close in size to him. Anareta glanced at Bui Nele. Her eyes were like a mongoose salivating at freshly laid eggs. Jone retrieved the glassware from his little brother, but not before a brief skirmish. Anareta watched with bated breath, unable to speak. She feared it would be the last time she laid eyes on her vase; either Bui Nele would needle her way into securing it for herself, or the boys would break it into irreparable pieces before their grand-aunt could get her hands on it.

"You know, I host a women's prayer group at home every Wednesday morning. That will look so good on my sitting room table. I must show the women that our service to God is not in vain. A beautiful vase will prove to them that God blesses His servants."

Anareta knew Bui Nele's sitting room only too well — her whole house, in fact. She had been there on the few occasions she visited her husband's village in the islands. It was like a hoarder's den; except that Bui Nele kept an immaculate home. Everything had its place. And she was a good conservator of space, stacking items in ways difficult to replicate. There was hardly any room to move around in Bui Nele's copious house. Every wall space was parked with pictures, both family photographs and paintings. There were certificates from Bui Nele's children's Primary School days pinned up with thumbtacks and *salusalu* garlands that had turned dark brown with age.

The sofas had decorative doormats covering the seats, armrests, and backrests. A large *masi* covered an entire sitting room wall and in each bedroom was a flag; the flag of Israel, a school flag, and the noble banner blue.

There was a special room where Bui Nele kept her mats. Mats for all occasions and mats in their numbers. They were stacked high, almost reaching the ceiling. Anareta dreaded what the room would smell like if a leak ever appeared on the roof.

Bui Nele's built-in kitchen cabinet housed cups and plates in the dozens, many for display purposes only and collecting dust. She even had more kitchen appliances than any modern kitchen Anareta had ever entered. Most remained unused. They sat like the display section of Brick-a-bracks at an Op-shop.

When Anareta finally left the congestion for some fresh air, she met her husband's distant cousin. "How's my rice cooker doing?" the cousin asked.

Anareta was confused at first. It was a strange way to be greeted. But when another woman asked a question along the same lines: I hope she's actually using that microwave she asked me for, did Anareta begin to put the pieces together. Most, if not all, the items in Bui Nele's home were given to her. Whether by goodwill or compulsion, Anareta could only conjecture. And it was only conjecture that Anareta could now rely on in estimating what Bui Nele would leave with after this visit.

"Come here, child, let me look at that vase," said Bui Nele. If she had the strength of youth, she would have reached her arm out in greedy anticipation. But now, she only beckoned with a slight wave of her hand.

Jone looked at his mother with uncertainty. Anareta gave a half-hearted nod. Bui Nele cradled the large vase on her lap like a newborn. She caressed the long neck down to the curve of the vase base.

"You know," she said, meeting Anareta's eyes before looking at the children one by one, "when you look after widows and orphans, you're doing it unto the Lord."

Anareta refrained from rolling her eyes. Her aunt-in-law pulled the widow card one too many times. Like the first time they had met at a soli to construct a new wing for the village church. The older woman had disarmed Anareta with her smile, the kind that could have graced billboards at Nadi International Airport.

"You must be Anareta, Lorima's wife," she said, after planting a kiss on Anareta's cheek. Anareta noticed Bui Nele's coiffed, soft hair, combed away from the ears and forehead. The smell of *mokosoi* and Kris perfumed body lotion lingered around her aunt-in-law. Anareta could tell that she had once been beautiful. She wasn't bad-looking now. But something had crept in, far less obvious than the wrinkles that appeared with age. Rather, an unsettling beneath the surface. Something Anareta knew she should be wary of.

"I'm sorry I couldn't make it to your wedding. We had a funeral," said Bui Nele. For a funeral is where wealth can be accumulated.

But Bui Nele had not spoken this out loud. At the soli, Bui Nele paid a visit to the hall kitchen where the women sat swatting flies away from large pots. They served food in deep bowls and long dishes. It was louder than a fish market on a Saturday in Suva City as the women joked amongst themselves, gossiped, and caught up on yesteryears. Anareta's attention was drawn to Bui Nele as the older woman beckoned her.

"What food do you have?" asked Bui Nele. Anareta gave her the rundown of dishes, as if Bui Nele hadn't just tasted the lot.

"My husband is sickly. You know how old people get when they're sick. They're fussy eaters. I don't think he'd like any of these. But what's that covered under the white cloth?"

The kitchen grew emptier as the nearby women joined the last of the diners in the main hall. Anareta removed the white covering from the pot. There was a whole piglet, golden brown and nestled in the sturdy plaits of coconut fronds.

"Yes," breathed Bui Nele. Her voice held the tone of someone who had found the holy grail. "My husband will love this. I'm telling you it will be the only thing he will eat from all the dishes here today."

Anareta was unsure. But Bui Nele was quick to belay her concerns.

"Look at all this food, my girl. Everyone's eaten. What's left is to take away." She patted the younger woman's back to make haste.

"Now hurry, my husband will be ravenous. He's waiting at home." Next, Bui Nele fished out a roll of tin foil from her bag.

"Here, wrap it in this to keep it extra warm."

The next few seconds went by in such a whirl that Anareta didn't have time to gawk and wonder what kind of woman would go to an event with a whole roll of aluminum foil tucked away in her bag.

But it would be a memory she would think back to often and one she would never witness again from another person. Stranger still was that Bui Nele wanted to wrap the roasted piglet again when it was already perfectly wrapped.

Yet Bui Nele didn't stop there. Instead, she selected several *dalo* baked to perfection and slipped everything into a large plastic bag. Then she left the kitchen without so much as a backward glance of gratitude to Anareta.

Half an hour later, when the woman running the kitchen came looking for the Reverend's lovo baked pork, she turned the kitchen upside down in her search.

"Where's the roasted piglet?" Anareta joined the commotion later when she returned from her meal.

She piped up, "I gave it to Bui Nele." There were curses flung all around. Anareta didn't know what the fuss was all about.

"The tidal wave has struck again," said an onlooker.

"Poor girl, don't blame her. She doesn't know that woman like we do," said another.

When the voices calmed down, Anareta said, "She said her husband was at home sick and that he wouldn't eat anything else but that pork."

The next comment made Anareta realise that she had just been duped. "She has no husband - she's a widow."

As all tidal waves do, they recede back into the bowels of the ocean. But they never go back empty-handed. Bui Nele, despite Anareta's efforts to hide things away, left with three baking trays, a sack of old newspapers (she said she would use it as wrapping paper for her fish business), bars of soap from Lorima's factory, a bunch of coconuts ...and the vase. Things weren't different this time around, after all.

"Just let her have it. She doesn't have anyone. Things are what give her meaning," Lorima said when Anareta told him he needed to speak to his aunt about her siphoning ways.

The truth was neither one of them could confront Bui Nele. It was against their culture. It was against their religion. Fear kept them silent. Fear of repercussions from on high for dishonouring an elder. Fear of gossip from the very same people who suffered alongside them. All they could really do was let the tidal wave go and hope it would not return too soon.

Several weeks after Bui Nele's visit, Lorima came home to relay some exciting news.

"I've got a new job. It pays three times my current one."

"What's the catch?" said Anareta.

"It's in Vatukoula." Anareta was not overjoyed by the sudden call to move to unfamiliar territory. However, the family's need for increased finance trumped her need for comfort and familiarity.

Eventually, time settled the Sekoula family into their new home in the northern highlands of the main island. And though they were away from their extended family, news always arrived sooner or later. They sat watching the evening news one day when a familiar face appeared on the screen. She was wiping tears from her aged eyes.

"Bui Nele!" cried Luisa and Jone in unison. Anareta hushed her children. Her husband turned the television volume up. "I've lost everything - EVERYTHING!" mourned Bui Nele. She had also lost a tooth since Anareta saw her last.

"The tidal wave came without warning. It took everything from me. I'm lucky to be alive. I only have the clothes on my back."

The camera panned to the remnants of Bui Nele's home. The house lay flattened. Several stray belongings, now flotsam and jetsam, littered the shoreline. A glint of light caught Anareta's eye.

There, whether intact or broken, she couldn't tell, for the bottom half was buried in sand, was her flower vase. She had long accepted the loss of the vase. She sighed with relief. Thank goodness tidal waves didn't reach that far inland.

STEPPING OUT

By Paulini Turagabeci

Most people like the warmth of the sun's early rays as it sifts through the tiny crack of two drawn curtains, not quite meeting. Most people like the song of the early bird, not quite seen among the leaves. Most people like the smell of hot roti on the tawa as it meets the air and melts the morning mist. But not Ema.

> *The sun scratches my eyes.*
> *Its harsh light extinguishes my black peace.*
> *Let me breathe.*
> *But I do not want to see.*
> *The smell of daylight is like inhaling sulphur.*
> *It rises up my throat*
> *Sizzle, gurgle, squirm.*

These days, Ema could barely open her eyes. The first ray of light streaming through her bedroom curtains burned itself into her retina. Gazing at the clock, she could tell it was still early. The only thing Ema could hear were the sounds of her two children playing in the living room. Against what she knew to be true, she wished that maybe the darkness behind her eyes would stick around when she opened them. But every time she did, it was morning. For Ema, it was more like mourning.

She dreaded the birdsong of predawn because it meant the sun would be out soon, and so would people.

If Ema had her way, she would bolt her doors, close every window, draw each curtain, and remain sequestered from the cacophony of the world. But life rarely went her way. She had two children to look after, and they loved the day.

Funny what six years can do to a person, for she wasn't always this way. Ema had been a housewife. She'd grown accustomed to the four walls of her one-bedroom home in Newtown. Her neighbourhood was densely populated. She knew the majority of her neighbours as they did her. But for the most part, Ema kept to herself, preferring instead to keep house, watch the daily Indian soap at midday while she ironed, then listen to some radio as she prepared dinner. It was a mundane life, but she had no complaints.

Today was different. Today, Ema had to go into town. She had a fitful sleep the night prior at the prospect of stepping into public. But sleep finally brought oblivion, albeit temporarily, until she woke up to dread again.

At 25, Ema was finally going to the first job

interview of her life.

She got the call a few days ago.

"I got a callback," said Ema. She clutched her phone tighter to keep her hands from trembling as she relayed the news to her mother-in-law, Taina.

"Hallelujah, *noqu lewa*. That's great news."

Great wasn't precisely the word Ema would use to describe whatever she was feeling in her heart and trying to come to terms with in her head. She didn't want to admit it, but some part of her wished she hadn't received the call at all. It meant she would need to leave the sanctuary of her home. She hated feeling that way. She was supposed to be happy that the cleaning company considered her application even if she had no prior experience.

She did meet the minimum qualification listed in Kara's copy of the Fiji Times though; Year 12 pass, able to do shift work, honest and reliable.

"Find something you're interested in?" said Kara, her next-door neighbour, as she took a long drag from her Benson & Hedges that Saturday morning.

Kara was five foot ten, a Naitasiri native with skin flawless and dark like rich coffee, natural hair cut short in the softest curls women paid big bucks to mimic with a perm. She was Naomi Campbell's doppelganger, but modeling was far from a career choice for Kara.

In the four years they had been neighbours, Ema never knew Kara's trade, nor did she broach the subject. She'd seen strange men spend the night in Kara's home but she refused to chase any insinuation down the rabbit hole. Whatever Kara's job was, she lived comfortably from it.

Kara had a large smart TV mounted on the wall to make room for other things in her small home. Her washing machine was large, the latest automatic model, and wasn't noisy. She even had a microwave oven; a luxury Ema couldn't even dream of.

Her home smelled of cheap perfume, overpowered only by the constant cling of cigarette smoke.

"I'd like to try out for this Maqosa Dina Cleaning Company," said Ema, pointing at the vacancy crammed into a small boxed border.

"Set," said Kara, who ground the stub of her cigarette in an ashtray. Her long purple acrylic nails looked like pincers ready to catch a tiny rodent. "Write your CV and cover letter, and I'll get Tomu to type it out on his laptop. Do you have a USB stick?"

Ema didn't. She hardly even knew how to use the new smartphone her mother-in-law sent from the States.

"Here, let me see that," said Kara, looking over Ema's shoulder to the job vacancy. "Oh, you don't need a USB at all. There's an email address there. You have an email, don't you?"

To this, Ema shook her head.

"No worries. I'll tell Tomu to set up your email account and you can use it in the future. He'll send in your application and give you the password."

Tomu was the male replica of his mother when it came to features, but he was the studious sort, locked away in front of a screen while his mother was rambunctious and worldly. Ema and Tomu hardly exchanged words as neighbours, now his mother was making him do Ema a favour.

Ema received a call three days after applying. She was both surprised and panicked.

"I'm sending some money to your M-Paisa. Withdraw it and buy something for work. Don't worry about the children. I'll send some money for them later," said Taina.

It was nearing midday in Fiji. California was 19 hours behind. Ema heard the familiar jingle-jangle of Taina's keys as she prepared to make her way to work, caring for a rich old Ella McDougal, a stubborn crank who lived alone without a friend or relative for company. She was the perfect candidate for Fijian women who went to California without proper papers. The women desperately hung on to a source of living and the old cranks couldn't scare them away with their volatility. In time, many desperate women and old cranks grew to rely on each other, maybe even liking each other.

Life had not favoured Ema, but she certainly won the lottery for mothers-in-law. Taina had been a solo parent, raising Poasa through the years, working in every factory in Suva; the biscuit factory, the flour factory, soap and detergent factory, garment factory, shoe factory, and even roofing iron factory.

Ema knew Taina was a strong woman, and for that reason, she couldn't disclose just how crippling the emotions in the pit of her stomach were.

"Just breathe, Ema," she told her reflection. She took a closer look at her pink lipstick and thought better of wearing makeup. Grabbing a baby wipe, she swiped her lips.

Ema felt deep dread uncurling itself in the pit of her stomach like a snake heightening before it strikes. Ema dressed her kids in silence. She couldn't let them see her fear.

The boys were in their usual attire: Alifereti in a pair of light blue jeans and a black pullover that said POLICE, Eminoni, black pants and a black hoodie that said THUG. You don't get to choose your labels when you don't have money. You let the designers express their worldview, then squeeze yourself into their pant legs and neck openings, hoping you fit in.

"Where we going Mummy?" said Alifereti, her four-year-old. He was picking up English quickly from the hours she let him spend in front of the screen. Ema felt guilty, but she didn't let him play outside and rarely did a peer come to visit.

"We're going to take a bus ride to town," said Ema, even as she felt her throat constricting as the words left her.

"Stay close, Reti," she said. She hoisted Eminoni high on her hips as she fumbled with the door keys.

Ema double-locked the door, tempted every time to return inside. But she willed herself to stride off along the cement footpath of her home and kept going until she reached the road.

Just one step in front of the other.
Jittery like a jolt of lightning searing through me.
Just breathe, keep moving, emasculated, aggravated.
Hold down the burning bile of breathless panic.
Swallow it and keep it trapped in your stomach.

The windowless bus blared local reggae remixes over the speakers. It seemed Ema's heart kept in time with the harsh clashing of the cymbals.

Clash closely to the source of disaster.
Mimic the sounds of my pandemonium.
Play purposefully with ill intent; bang, clang, gong,
goes your song.

The bus made its usual commute around the winding streets of Newtown. A group of boys who had known her husband got on at the corner shop.

Ema wanted to hide for no good reason.

"Sista, Bula," said one of the boys with a warm smile. Another boy handed Alifereti a stick of gum as he passed by. The young men looked Ema in the eyes and nodded a silent greeting at least as they made their way to the back of the bus. The last thing anyone did was accuse her of her husband's incarceration.

Everyone knew the truth about that night. Poasa had heard the commotion outdoors. A brawl had broken out during a drinking party. He ran out to stop it. He singled out the perpetrator and while others had hassled the drunk man, it was Poasa's blow that landed him on the ground, never to get up again. The charge against Poasa was manslaughter; the final verdict - a minimum time of ten years, with no chance of probation before five.

The judge moved on to the next case, the lawyers moved on to their next client, the police moved on to their next complaint, even the victims family had buried their dead and moved on. But Ema was left alone with broken pieces of an incomplete home, scrambling to piece together the life she once knew.

All the years she'd lived in ignorant bliss, away from the world, was stripped away from her. She had to be both mother and father to her children. She had to be the breadwinner.

The bus lurched to a noisy stop at the Suva bus

stand. Alifereti's eyes lit up in wonder at the life around him. It all seemed so new to him because the last time he had been there was before his father went to prison. Eminoni, too squirmed on his mother's lap, eager to follow the other passengers out of the bus. The boys from the corner shop helped Ema with her sons. They carried Alifereti and Eminoni outside and set them on the hard pavement of Suva's bus bay. Ema said an awkward "Vinaka" for their help before they moved off.

It was strange. Ema had been to Australia once, a long time ago. Everything had been new, peculiar, unfamiliar, in an exciting way. It was expected. A new place. New faces. The comfort of obscurity was like the act of snuggling under a cosy blanket on a rainy day. Ema could be herself, do what she wanted, and be left to exist.

But here, in familiar territory, she saw Bas Deo the bean-seller, peddling his wares of tightly packed bean, peanuts, and saio's, as he wove between buses and people, his basket held effortlessly in the crook of an elbow. He called out, "Bean-peanut, Peanut-bean, Bean-peanut," in a hypnotic lyrical drone.

Once in a while, Bas Deo would sit, split open a packet and scatter the savory contents on the grease-smeared bus stand tarmac. Flocks of pigeons descended in droves and pecked vigorously at Bas Deo's offering.

Ema was familiar with the local dialects spoken

around her. She overheard a woman berating her husband over the phone in the Yasawa dialect. Something about only giving $300 for funeral arrangements instead of the $600 his relatives were demanding.

In the distance, at the Western bus bay, bara boys raced alongside the buses that came to berth, bringing their wheelbarrows dangerously close to the bus wheels. Their shouts carried on the wind, the same wind that picked up a stray newspaper page here and a corn husk there.

Everything was familiar to Ema. There was nothing new under the Suva City Sun. Yet, despite the familiarity, she still felt out of place, like an unwelcome foreigner. Like she didn't belong, but without promise that she even belonged elsewhere....somewhere. It was strange.

Ema couldn't look at anybody, couldn't make eye contact. She didn't want to feel the pity in people's eyes. She was ashamed of being a single mother. Despite reminding herself that no one knew her circumstance, neither would they care, she felt palpable shame and disappointment at her lot in life just the same.

Flipetty flap descends the wings of shame.
Hide me in your dark embrace.
Cough, breathe, cough, inhale the exhaust of wasted days.
Cement my weighted feet to the ground when all I

want to do is run.

Ema's grip on Noni was vice-like. Perched on her hips, it was almost as if he was her human shield, drawing him closer whenever anybody drew near, both to keep him from colliding with another human being, but more to protect herself. From what? She didn't know.

At the back of her mind and in the core of her being, Ema believed the world to be a cruel place, and while she could still shield her sons from it, she would.

She wouldn't buy new shoes. New shoes often meant blisters and she couldn't afford to get those early into her job. Instead, she would wear her black pumps—the one she had worn for years but was still in good condition. A part of her was superstitious. Maybe it would bring her good luck.

Ema and the boys went to the Vodafone outlet at MHCC to withdraw the money. The air-conditioning was a good respite from the outdoor humidity, but it did little to ease Ema's tension among a crowd.

When she had received the money, they headed to the shoeshine boys to shine her shoes. She looked at the row of boys seated on low stools, bent over a customers shoe. Ema was unable to control where her thoughts wandered. These boys had once been as small as her Alifereti and Eminoni. Now they lived on the streets, hoping to make a decent living polishing people's shoes. What if her boys ended up on the streets? What if no one loved them enough to house them? What if all their youth was used up struggling to survive but never truly living? The thought alone terrified her. She watched an approaching bus to keep her eyes from breaking out in tears.

Value City at the old Regal Centre opened for new stock. But there was a long line of customers snaking around the building. The last thing Ema wanted to do was stand around people who might offer her small talk - or worse yet, deeper conversation. Besides, Ema didn't like crowds. She would also save money, money she could use on cheap food that would feed them for half a week.

So they headed to Bargain Box on Nina street instead. The second-hand clothing store was holding a half-price sale. Alifereti and Eminoni played with toy cars at the toy section while Ema rummaged through the aisle of skirts hanging in loose, gapped lines on welded steel rods. All the nice skirts were taken. But she wasn't looking for nice. She was looking for "wearable." As long as it was black, didn't have a hole, and she could afford it, it would do.

Taina would have scolded her. "Why don't you buy something nice for yourself for a change? You're always thinking about everyone else like it's a crime to have nice things."

Thank goodness her mother-in-law was five and a half thousand miles away to know the difference.

"Why don't you try this one? I think it will look good on you."

Ema looked up from her place at the narrow mirror. The skirt she had chosen was a size too big and the hem was already fraying. She was figuring out how to make adjustments to it at home.

An older lady held out a midi pencil skirt. Ema felt her cheeks burn. She couldn't wear that. But it seemed the woman read her mind.

"It will look better on you than me, trust me," said the woman.

This time Ema went into the fitting room instead of holding the skirt to her waist at the mirror outside. The woman was right. The skirt fit perfectly. She turned from side to side, nervous that it would bring attention to her behind.

"Mummy, can I come inside?"

It was Eminoni.

"Hang on, Noni, I'm coming out."

Eminoni giggled when he saw his mother in the pencil skirt. Ema panicked.

"Doesn't she look nice and smart?" said the woman who had taken the liberty to wait to see how the skirt looked on Ema.

"Wow, Mummy," said Alifereti who joined the small crowd of onlookers.

Ema looked at herself once more in the mirror before packing the skirt away. Finding a blouse was easier. She settled for a white one with elbow-length sleeves. She was happy with her purchase.

She had all she needed for the interview. There was money left over to bring a cousin from the village to look after her boys when she was at work. She flipped through the colourful bills in her purse; blue, yellow, green, red. There was enough for a week's groceries and a week's bus fare to work, which she'd need to top up her e-ticketing card. There was also enough for a new toy for the boys and lunch.

Ema avoided crowded places. She was terrible at chit-chat. Even a friendly Bula found it hard to escape the confines of her dry, constricted throat. She didn't know when she became this withdrawn, frail leaf of a woman. She had been a tree climber, a rock thrower, a people hugger, and a reliable friend as a child.

They hate me.
They're cruel.
Faceless, nameless bodies crowd around me.
They hate me for no reason.

Ema bought roti parcels from a dark Chinese fast

food diner and a large bottle of Frubu to go. Ema led her boys to the embankment behind Village 6 cinemas.

The boys' voices rose with excitement. Ema's heart ached at the thought of not being able to afford to take them to the beach.

A mother and her three children sat near her. Her children played together with Ema's boys. It gave Ema hope that not everyone was out to harm her.

Despite Ema's attempts to keep her boys within the invisible lines of their boundary, Alifereti and Eminoni gravitated to the children and soon they were playing He, laughing, falling and getting up again. But when the boys accepted their friend's offer of Pizza and Coke, Ema was embarrassed. She tried to reel them away with a disapproving stare.

"It's okay. There's plenty to go around," said the children's mother. She extended a hand of pizza to Ema.

"Please, have some roti," said Ema. The woman received it in a mutual show of camaraderie.

"Sukuna Park is crowded today. But we prefer it here. The kids like to feed the fish," said the woman.

What Ema really wanted to say was, "Thank you for being kind to my kids." But it didn't suit the occasion and she didn't really have anything to say. So the two families sat there for a while; the children continued their games while the women enjoyed each other's company in silence.

This time, as they made their way back to the bus stand, Ema felt a little lighter around the head, where once she was bogged down with thoughts that saw the world awash in tones of grey. Her stomach too did not recoil in dread and the freedom travelled down to her feet, making her steps seem more buoyant. She was vigilant though. Bliss was temporary until the wet blanket of dread hovered over you again. But until then, Ema decided to live. When the fight came, she would fight.

Maybe the world wouldn't be as scary for her and her boys after all. One day when her sons would make their way through life on their own, they would find caring strangers not out to harm them.

Serenity is blue.
Like the sea.
Like the sky.
On a windless, cloudless day.
But when a breeze picks up, breathe.
Let it dance on the skin of my forearm and play under the sun
Smell the smile of life.
Release the black tendrils of smoke that linger in my veins.

Tomorrow, she would step out in confidence for her interview and she would continue to do so the day after that and the day after that. Until the day that her husband stepped out of jail too.

THE THIRD PRIZE

By Khemendra Kumar

Friday afternoon. Sanjay sat on the threshold of his home: a house at the heart of Lowcost Housing. Legs outstretched on the bevel stairs; he showed the level of propriety of a gatekeeper. On his lap, he balanced an aged tin box case inherited from his elder brother - Ganesh. Eventually the box case showed its detachment from this world; the outer layer began to peel off from all corners as if a dog suffering from mange. But the sordid look of the box case didn't matter to Sanjay. What mattered most was that it housed his most precious toys and mementos: a broken tooth, a small HB pencil, a drawing book, his toy truck, and his milk bottle with the well-used silicone nipple still attached. In his secret games, he pretended to suckle milk from this bottle like a baby. This box case also held Sanjay's dreams: dreams that were captured in his drawing book.

On top of his aged box case, Sanjay placed a book on display. His Third Prize in Class One! It was a storybook. Jack and The Beanstalk—a hardcover

Penguin Classic with double bind spine. The front cover displayed a wide-eyed boy in rags climbing the winding beanstalk. The back cover promoted the many other fairy tales offered by the publisher. Now, this is a keeper! This was the biggest achievement of Sanjay's life to date. Obviously, he had a sound reason to be happy. Happiness was painted all over his face.

Sanjay flipped open the cover many times, each time unable to take his eyes off a sticker. The sticker was a template and it read:

Sanjay Lal
Class 1B
Third Prize
Bulileka Primary School

He admired the way his name was imprinted–neat slants and smooth curves; it seemed to be calligraphed by a machine. But no. That was his Teacher Jee's handwriting. He sometimes sneaked a peek into her workbook to admire her handwriting.

Sanjay kept fidgeting with the book. He turned the cover page again and again, closed it, and then looked hard at the back cover. He traced the beanstalk upwards, gently feeling the shiny plastic coat. He held his book close to his nose and sniffled. It smelt new. With his thumb and index finger, Sanjay measured the thickness of the cover. Never had he held a book with such a measure. An insatiable desire to peel the plastic and peep inside the thickness popped up in his mind. But he withheld his emotion. On second thought, he licked the plastic coating.

Sanjay was immensely pleased. He alternated these actions. Tired of fidgeting, he flipped through all the pages to look at the black prints and the colourful illustrations. Sanjay didn't care much to read the story, not that he was a poor reader: he had heard this tale numerous times after lunch at school. Teacher Jee religiously narrated two stories: Cinderella and Jack and the Beanstalk. Cinderella didn't make much sense to him. But he enjoyed Jack's tale. Although small, Jack, with all the loot, managed to run away from the giant. That was astounding! Sanjay liked the running episode the most. He himself enjoyed running. He was least bothered about other things in school. But during recess and lunch, Sanjay ran. He ran to the tap; he ran to the toilet; he ran around the classroom block, and he ran around the peepal[1] tree believed to host a sacred snake near the Ram Mandir. He also ran from post to post of the Lankapuri[2]: a shelter for Ravana[3] during the annual Ramleela[4]. During sports, he ran after the soccer ball, occasionally running ahead of the ball, to the dismay of his team, and the amusement of the others. Binnu, his childhood friend, couldn't help but run with him, run away from him, or run after him. Sanjay practically ran wherever his thin bowlegs could carry him. Soon he was recognised as the 'Boy with wheels.'

With such fame, he was sure to become adventurous, trying new running styles. Sanjay tried sprints, lazy running, stop-start, sudden take-off, cutting acute corners, and whatnot. He imitated the monkey-faced bus snaking up Rice Mill Road, huffing and puffing, or Cinappa's sugarcane truck groaning under a full load along the cemetery. Once he became a taxi, Morning Jay's taxi, to be precise.

"If one is to be a taxi, better be Morning Jay's," he thought. It was common knowledge in Labasa that Morning Jay's Nissan Cedric sped like a wild beast and he never failed to display the power of his car, especially to his rivals–The Lucky Brothers with a fleet of Datsun 120Y.

But Sanjay was unlucky on that day. He failed to negotiate the football metal goalpost. Dhummm! He crashed into the post. Immediately, his headlights turned black and blue while the side fender faced many dents. He was taken to Master Moti Lal to receive first aid. Moti Lal generously applied yellow iodine on the bruises. The iodine burned through his skin. The strong smell travelled from Sanjay's nose to the inside of his head. He felt nauseated for a little while. After treatment, the right side of his face looked like a rotten ripe pumpkin. Once done with the first aid, Moti Lal firmly gripped the belt loops of Sanjay's khaki pants with his scaly fingers and dragged him closer to himself, close enough for

Sanjay to see the tunnels of Moti Lal's bushy nostrils. Without warning, Moti Lal's heavy palm landed on Sanjay's left cheek. Chataak! Immediately, the left side of Morning Jay's taxi turned red.

"Get lost from my eyes, you Lilliput!" Moti Lal roared as Sanjay scooted away.

Back at home, he received similar treatment of various degrees. Never try goofy running, Sanjay promised himself, but as his bruises healed, he backtracked to his old habits. It was settled. Nothing could stop Sanjay. But today he was sitting in the same spot, and that was for quite some time. The reason was simple. He wanted to show his singular achievement to his father. And so, patiently, he waited for his father.

The threshold is a border that controls inside-outside conflicts. Sanjay's sitting on that border annoyed the right wing. Ajji[5] walked past him, her white cotton lehenga[6] gently tailing her. She could have been easily taken for an Indian chief. Her tantrums were very noble. But fate smeared her skin with copper, her father crossed kalapani[7] on the Sutlej, and the rest is the distorted history of a subaltern.

"Oye, what happen Sanjay? You sitting like a bag of bhusa[8], tell me, is everything all right? Did you break a leg or what?" she asked enquiringly.

"No leg break Ajji, I am fit. Ajji, look... I get a prize, third prize!" Sanjay exclaimed. Ajji halted to have a good look. She narrowed her eyebrows and strained her eyes.

"Why you never come to see me get prize!" he questioned her in the same breath.

"You get a prize! me full surprise, I never see you read a single page, always running, check see this book, maybe the prize for your running wild." She reasoned out loudly. She walked back into her room with an air of disbelief.

"Pura kalyug[9] hai, now even donkeys chew cashew nuts," was Ajji's witty comment. "And your mother never tell me, maybe she don't want me come," she whipped out of her room. The outburst was loud enough for the left wing. Mother banged her door shut.

Sanjay was miffed momentarily. But soon he recomposed himself.

"There is a good reason Ajja[10] has named her Mahadevi[11]." He thought. "What does she know about school, only thing she can read is that book–Mahabharat[12]," he added to the initial thought. It was assumed in the past that Mahabharat invited conflicts in the family. Ajja tried very hard to extort the name of the person who gifted Ajji this sacred book. Ajji kept the gifter's name secret while Ajja promised himself to pound the secret gifter, just like the way Bhima[13] pounded Jatasura[14].

No sooner Sanjay saw his Ajja walking back home. He walked like a Bengali tiger, ready to pounce on anyone who vexed him. Well–not everyone. Ajji had domesticated him long ago. In front of Ajji, he was a soft-pawed kitten.

As he approached, Sanjay paid him obeisance.

"Ram Ram[15] Ajja," Without waiting for a reply, Sanjay blurted out, "Ajji was asking for you, she wants some suluka[16] leaves to smoke," he informed him nonchalantly. At this old age, Ajji smoked incessantly. Her mosquito net was like a quarantine chamber. Even Ajja, who chewed sukhi[17] all his life, found the room unbearable.

"Your Ajji big cranky now, day and night smoking suluka and reading loud," Ajja responded with annoyance. "Anyway, why you sitting at the door? Don't you know you are inviting evil spirits? Go inside gachu[18] before Ajji sees you," he cautioned. Superstition was next to religion at their home.

"Acha[19] I will, but first look at this." Sanjay showed his book. He didn't let Ajja hold his book with those soiled hands.

"I won't gobble that book of yours," Ajja said, dismissing Sanjay's sense of possession. "Show me —English sahib book, behaal hai[20]! You sing Babba Black Sheepa, you are smart but how you smart yourself, only God knows. You full time running like a bush horse ehh," Ajja cast doubt and appreciation simultaneously.

A puzzled look clouded Ajja's face. None of his

children ever got to finish primary school. He thought hard. His thinking was clear on his aging face. As said earlier, Ajja was a man of might, less of mind. Negotiating his weakness, he stopped thinking hard and offered to buy Sanjay a lali mithai[21] at Poni's shop as a treat.

Tempting as it was, Sanjay declined but asked gingerly, "Ajja, why you never come to school?"

"Aree[22], you know, I was at Lal Bihari's farm picking boda[23] beans. He sent a message to come and pick before the beans harden," Ajja reasoned but failed himself. He didn't reveal that Ajji sent him to labour on the farm in return for two bundles of boda beans. He sat on the ground and rested for a while. Suddenly, he started feeling inside the right-hand pocket of his trousers. He dug deep and brought out a five-cent coin.

Ajja flipped that coin to Sanjay and lovingly said, "buy something to eat."

Quick as a flash, Sanjay grabbed it, opened his tin box case, dropped the coin in, and immediately shut the lid. "Just in case Ajja changed his mind," Sanjay reasoned with himself. He also felt a little compensated.

As Ajja stood up to go Sanjay said, "I will show this book to Father." Ajja felt quite pleased with little Sanjay's thought.

Sanjay glanced at the wall clock. He realized the

wall clock was dysfunctional. The clock's hands fractured exactly at 10 o'clock a long time ago, but the pendulum kept swinging. Unperturbed Sanjay continued to wait. While waiting, he decided to explore his book further. He trailed the tendrils of the beanstalk on the cover page with his small index finger, being very careful not to scratch the smooth plastic coat with his fingernail. The beanstalk climbed higher and higher until engulfed by the white clouds. Sanjay looked up to see how the clouds looked in his part of the world. Far away, he saw a swirl of dust.

That was Ganesh, his elder brother, on a cycle. Ganesh paddled furiously, racing with the twilight. He was supposed to reach home way earlier. As usual, he was late. On many occasions, his habit of wanderlust got him into trouble. Last month, while cycling at night, he rammed into a parked sugarcane truck. For a week, Ganesh walked around nursing a black eye.

Just a few meters before the stairs, he jammed the brakes of his cycle–the Hercules. The Hercules skidded on the patch of grass before coming to a halt. As soon as he got off, Ganesh chained the Hercules to the wooden stilts of the house. He took out a small bottle of machine oil from a rusty toolbox and carefully oiled the hub of the wheels. Once done, he lifted each wheel of the Hercules and spun. Once satisfied with caring for his cycle, he turned to Sanjay.

"Dekha[24]. How smooth this cycle runs?" he asked rhetorically. "This is Hercules mann… Hercules!" Ganesh claimed proudly.

The cycle had a proper name. Not only was the name embossed on the frame, but Ganesh had also written the name on the back of the rear mud flap using white paint. Other than the mythical name, the cycle was cursed. The Hercules was heavy and slow, like Ram Lal's old tractor. Most of the time, the Hercules ended up puncturing halfway to its destination. Other times, the brakes failed. Once the front wheel came out itself. Out of frustration, Ajja gave the cycle to Ganesh, hoping to eliminate the curse. But to Ganesh, the Hercules became a prized possession. Proprietorship in a pauper's house is taken seriously. Little things count, some say.

But talk we all can. And hearing these hollow praises made Sanjay giggle.

This moment deserved a brotherly mash-up. "Bhaiya[25], even I can outrun your cycle," Sanjay taunted.

"You wait, I will wipe that smirk off your face. Didn't you see me! I was flying boy, flying like…" Ganesh searched for a suitable word in his mental dictionary.

"Flying like a gadura[26] at night," Sanjay completed the sentence. Both brothers laughed out loud.

"Why you sitting at the door like Sudunai[27]?" Ganesh enquired gingerly.

"I am waiting for Father," Sanjay answered as a matter of fact. "Aree haa, Mother wants you to light the Tilly lamp. FEA wala falla[28] cut-off power today," Sanjay briefed Ganesh.

Ganesh came and sat beside Sanjay. For a moment both were quiet. Ganesh caught the shine of Sanjay's book. "Who gave you this book?"

"Bhaiya, I came third, this my prize. You should have come, nobody from home came," in saying so Sanjay not so willingly handed his book to Ganesh. Ganesh was back-paddling now.

"Boyo boy, now I know why your tongue snips like scissors. You are not bhondo[29] boy. You are the fast one," he wholeheartedly praised Sanjay, "come I take you for a double bunk." Ganesh offered a ride.

"No bhaiya, remember... last time I ended up in the bougainvillea plant. Three thorns pierced my bum, no fear... never sit double bunk with you," Sanjay replied curtly.

Ganesh couldn't stop laughing. He reasoned that both should get in the house before Mother laced their backs with the sasa[30] broom.

The Tilly lamp was lit and hung at the door. The dim light attracted all the family members to the living room, like moths. All animosity disappeared in the darkness and the singular motive of waiting for Father began.

It was past seven, Sanjay guessed. Darkness engulfed the small home. Mother went to the makeshift kitchen and dished food in two plates— one for me and one for herself. In the dim light, he saw brown rice, dhal, a small piece of motee roti[31], and a lump of coconut chutney. It was the Friday menu and was prepared to the liking of Sanjay's Father.

Father was a prodigal son who returned every Friday from his banwaas[32]. Not only did he return, but he also brought happiness in the form of his wages. Though meager, Mother managed the entire week with that wage, waiting for another Friday. But today, Mother was unusually quiet, her stress dug deep near her temples, black scars appeared under her eyelids, and her eyes were doleful. She sat like a dasi[33] in the Ramleela[34].

Father had worked at the Agriculture Station in Dreketi after his lay-off from the Colonial Sugar Refinery. So, he shifted the location from one colonial set-up to another outpost. This outpost was hospitable though. Like a patient, Father was allocated a single wooden bed in a shared room in the barrack. The room measured eight by ten feet, almost the size of the rooms the girmitiyas[35] occupied in the coolie lines[36]. Unlike the girmitiyas, Father returned home every Friday; unlike the girmitiyas, Father's girmit would end upon his retirement from work after twenty-six years.

They all knew Father would arrive late but that did not deter them from waiting for him. Even Tommy, the flea-infested mongrel, sat patiently at the door, whimpering occasionally. Who knows on which Friday Father would surprise them? With this singular hope, they sat in a semi-circle facing the main door. That door was their window. They all were in one way wanting to cross the threshold of poverty, but this home had some magic that bound their feet.

The silence was punctuated with a little talk. Ajja signalled to Ganesh asking if he had pounded the lavena[37] he had bought.

Ajji quizzed about the taste of the chutney. "Just one coconut you know, otherwise I could make gari mithai[38] for you, next time... for you third prize," she casually promised.

Turning to his mother, Sanjay said, "Ma, why didn't you come to school? All parents came. No one was there standing beside me," Sanjay said with suppressed sobs.

Mother looked around. All the adult eyes stole away from her questioning eyes. But the innocent heart needed an answer.

"Just as I was about to leave home, the FEA wala falla came. He cut the power supply," Mother said guardedly. "In all this jhanjhat[39], I got late."

"But why Ma, he never cut badka appa's[40] power supply?" Sanjay rebutted. Mother crouched like a hermit crab to hide in her imaginary shell. But she failed to do so. She also failed to suppress her tears that shone like pearls in the dim light of the Tilly lamp.

Ganesh intervened, "Oye smarty pants, give your book, I read this story to you." Cheerfully, Sanjay leaned on his brother's strong shoulders and heard Jack's tale till the end. His mind wandered in between as well. He imagined his father chasing the FEA wala falla with a sasa broom. Soon he was lost in his deep sleep. Ganesh gently picked him up and laid him on his bed. Then he put Jack and the Beanstalk inside the tin box case and closed it tight.

ABOUT THE AUTHORS

Khemendra Kamal Kumar

Khemendra Kamal Kumar is from Bulileka, Labasa. He lives in Lautoka and works at the Fiji National University as a lecturer. Earlier, he taught at the Lautoka Teachers' College and primary schools. His interest lies in literacy, children's literature, and English literature. He has published journal articles and written poems, short stories, and children's books. Currently, he is working on his second collection of poetry and short stories.

Paulini Turagabeci

Paulini Turagabeci is a writer and publisher known for her compelling and unique literary works. Born and raised in Fiji, she draws inspiration from her homeland, its people, and its legends. Her passion for writing led her to publish her first novel, "The River," a poignant story of love and loss that captured the hearts of readers. Her subsequent novels, "One to borrow, one to fake, one to consummate" and "Adi Qalau - A retelling of the Legend of the Tagimoucia," showcased her versatility as a writer and further established her as a rising talent in the literary world. Through her works, she explores themes of love, identity, culture, and the human experience, weaving together intricate plots and rich characters. Outside of writing, Paulini enjoys knitting and is often found sipping coffee as she works on her latest projects. Her dream is to one day meet her favorite author, Francine Rivers, and exchange ideas on the craft of writing.

---

[1] A fig tree.

[2] The capital of Lanka in the mythological Hindu epic Ramayana. The place where Ravana is housed while enacting Ramleela.

[3] A character in the Hindu epic Ramayana. Evil king of Lanka.

[4] An enactment of the Hindu epic Ramayana.

[5] Grandmother from the paternal side.

[6] Lehenga - ankle-length skirt.

[7] Black Water- refers to a past proscription of crossing the ocean in the Hindu culture.

[8] Husk/straw

[9] Kaliyuga/ Dark Age – the last of the four stages the world goes through as prescribed in the Sanskrit scriptures.

[10] Grandfather from the paternal side.

[11] The Hindu Goddess that is the sum of all other goddesses.

[12] Mahabharata- Ancient Hindi epic also 'the great tale of the Bharata dynasty.'

[13] The second son of Pandava in the Hindu epic Mahabharata known for his might and appetite.

[14] A demon who possessed power of illusion in the Hindu epic Mahabharata.

[15] A Hindu greeting

[16] Pandanus leaf

[17] Dried tobacco leaves

[18] Donkey

[19] Okay

[20] Impressive- an expression meaning very good in Fiji-Hindi.

[21] Lolly

[22] Oh! well

[23] Cow peas

[24] See!

[25] Brother

[26] Bat

[27] A local madman

[28] Person in charge of connecting and disconnecting electricity.

[29] Slob

[30] Fijian style broom

[31] Indian bread

[32] Exile as in mythical sense

[33] Servant

[34] The performance of Ramayana

[35] Indentured labourers

[36] Barracks

[37] Dried stem of a yagona plant.

[38] A sweet made from coconut meat.

[39] Trouble

[40] Father's elder brother or cousin

www.ingramcontent.com/pod-product-compliance
Lightning Source LLC
Chambersburg PA
CBHW071215130726
47998CB00002B/755